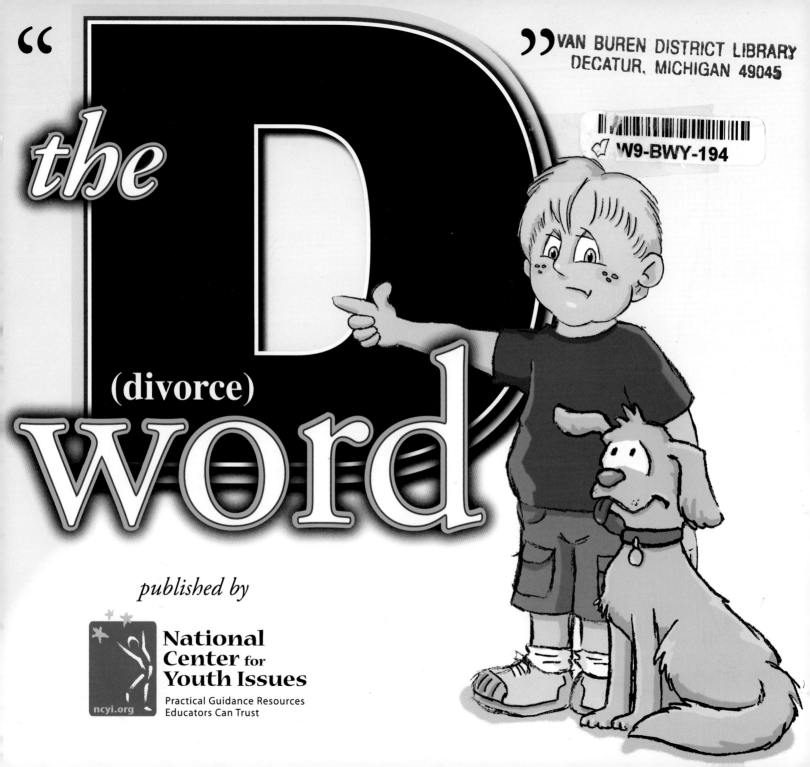

"the D (divorce) word"

published by

National Center for Youth Issues
Practical Guidance Resources
Educators Can Trust

ncyi.org

To Chelsey, Olivia, and Ella.
-Julia

Duplication and Copyright

National Center for Youth Issues
Practical Guidance Resources
Educators Can Trust

ncyi.org

P.O. Box 22185
Chattanooga, TN 37422-2185
423.899.5714 • 800.477.8277
fax: 423.899.4547
www.ncyi.org

ISBN: 978-1-931636-76-6
© 2011 National Center for Youth Issues, Chattanooga, TN
All rights reserved.

Written by: Julia Cook
Illustrations by: Phillip W. Rodgers
Published by National Center for Youth Issues
Softcover

Printed at RR Donnelley • Reynosa, Tamaulipas, Mexico • June 2011

Introduction

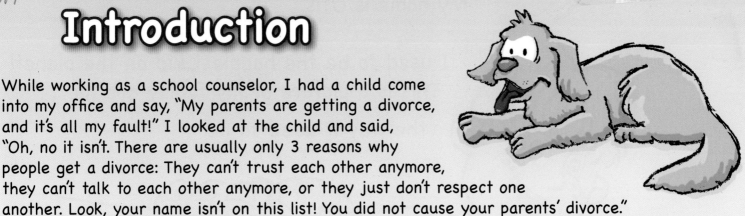

While working as a school counselor, I had a child come into my office and say, "My parents are getting a divorce, and it's all my fault!" I looked at the child and said, "Oh, no it isn't. There are usually only 3 reasons why people get a divorce: They can't trust each other anymore, they can't talk to each other anymore, or they just don't respect one another. Look, your name isn't on this list! You did not cause your parents' divorce."

When a family goes through a divorce, it can be stressful, confusing and difficult for everyone involved. In an attempt to make sense of the divorce, a child may place blame on him or herself.

The purpose of this book is to present a concrete explanation of why people get divorced and explain the three C's of divorce:

I did not **CAUSE** it.

I cannot **CONTROL** it.

I'm going to have to learn to **COPE** with it.

Successfully working through a divorce is a team effort. It's not always easy, but it can be done. Here are a few tips:

Divorce Survival Tips for Good Parents:

- Stay involved in your child's life in every way possible.
- Use direct communication with your ex-spouse – do not talk through your child.
- Do not say mean things about your ex-spouse in front of your child.
- Work hard to be civil to one another when your child is present.
- Support the time your child spends with your ex-spouse. Do not act jealous.
- Keep your child's teacher, school counselor, and child care provider informed.

BEST!

Julia Cook

My name is Otis.

I used to be the happiest kid on the planet!
This is a picture of my family and me...

the way it **used** to be.

When I was little, my
mom and dad were
best friends.

This is what my family looks like now. My mom won't even talk to my dad, and my dad won't even talk to my mom.

Sometimes, they both treat me more like a friend than one of their kids. I kinda like that, but I know that's not the way it's supposed to be.

I want things to be the way they used to be, but that won't happen...because my parents are getting a D...D...D...., the "D" word.

I can't even say it!

Today, I went to visit my Gram.
"I feel like it's all my fault," I said to her.

"Maybe if I had been a better kid, I'd still be happy."

"Why do you think that, Otis?"
Gram asked.

"**If...** I hadn't fought with Raymond and Ronald so much."

"**If...** I had studied harder for my spelling test."

"**Even if**... you had been nicer to Raymond and Ronald,

Even if... you had studied hard for every single spelling test,

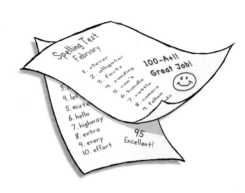

Even if... you hadn't put gum in Matilda Bruno's hair,

Even if... you had taken a bath every single time your mom told you to.

Your parents **would still** be getting a divorce."

"Otis," my Gram said. **"You can't control a divorce. It won't work.**

You are still a family, it's just now you are a different kind of family."

"Yeah," I said. "A D...D...D, the "D" word family. I can't even say it!"

"How can they do this to me? Don't they love me enough to stay together?"

"Of course they love you Otis! In fact, they probably love you now more than ever. The problem is that they are not in love with each other."

"It just isn't fair!"

"You're right," said Gram. *"It isn't fair, but the only thing that you can do is figure out a way to cope. This divorce is not going away so you are just going to have to learn to how deal with it!"*

"So what do I need to do?" I asked.

*"First of all, tell both of your parents that you don't like being **The Family Messenger**. They need to figure out a way to talk to each other and not make you talk for them."*

"How do I do that?
I don't want them to get mad at me."

"Find a good time to talk with each of them alone. They might not even realize how they are making you feel."

"What if I'm too **scared** to talk to them?"

*"Try drawing a picture or writing a letter that will tell them
how uncomfortable you feel when you are stuck in the middle."*

"What if I'm too afraid to tell them?"

"Try drawing a picture or writing a letter
that will tell them how you feel.

If that doesn't work, I will talk to both of them myself!"

"This divorce has not only been tough on you, it has also been really hard on your twin brothers. Do your best to be nicer to them and try not to fight so much. The three of you need to stick together.

Your parents are going through a lot right now too, and sometimes they might not act the way parents should. Set a good example for Raymond and Ronald by making good choices, even when your parents aren't around to tell you what to do."

"Otis, you don't have control over your parent's divorce, but you do have control over yourself.

Take your control in a positive direction. Just because your parents are getting divorced doesn't mean that you should divorce school.

Do your best to get good grades. Study hard for all of your tests... especially spelling!"

"Do everything you can to stay out of trouble at school...
You can start by leaving your gum at home!

Never use this divorce as an excuse for poor choices.
You will only hurt yourself if you do that."

I went back home and started to think about all of the things my Gram had said.

I'll probably never be able to say the D...D...D..."D" word, and things are never going to be like they used to be, but what my Gram told me does make sense.

I didn't
CAUSE it.

I can't
CONTROL it.

So I guess I'll
just have to learn
to **COPE** with it.

I think I'll go take a bath.

Just because the "D" word stinks,
doesn't mean that I have to.

More GREAT books from Julia Cook!!

Melvin the Magnificent Molar
By Julia Cook and Dr. Laura Jana
Melvin explains maintaining a healthy smile. This book highlights the importance of taking care of baby (primary) teeth by visiting the dentist every 6 months beginning at the age of one; when to use and how much fluoride toothpaste to use; and what to expect during a trip to see the dentist and dental hygienist.

My Mouth is a Volcano!
By Julia Cook
Louis always interrupts! But when others begin to interrupt Louis, he learns how to respectfully wait for his turn to talk. This book provides an empathetic approach to the habit of interrupting and teaches children a witty technique to help them manage their rambunctious thoughts and words.

Personal Space Camp
By Julia Cook
Louis is back! He's delighted to learn that his teacher has sent him to the principal's office to attend Personal Space Camp. Eager to learn more about lunar landings, space suits, and other cosmic concepts, Louis soon discovers that he has much to learn about personal space right here on earth.

Bully B.E.A.N.S.
By Julia Cook
A fun story that teaches people of all ages to become proactive when it comes to bullying. This book can help children and adults understand why bullying happens and what they can do to stop it. Finally, a bullying book that speaks to the bystander!

I Am A Booger...Treat Me With Respect!
By Julia Cook
Boogie the booger teaches the healthy way to blow your nose using a Booger Ghost. Boogie knows that most people think he's gross, but he doesn't feel bad because he keeps us from getting sick.

The Bubble Wrap Queen
By Julia Cook
This book teaches the key B.A.S.I.C.S of injury prevention. It reminds children and parents of important precautions to play and live safely...outside of the bubblewrap!

It's Hard To Be A Verb!
By Julia Cook
This adorable book teaches children with ADHD that it is sometimes hard to be a verb, but they just have to focus. It teaches kids how to wiggle their wiggles before the wiggles wiggle them and that being a verb is not their fault.

A Bad Case of Tattle Tongue
By Julia Cook
"Josh the Tattler" tattles way too much. One night he wakes up to find his tongue is very long, yellow, and covered in bright purple spots. Will a bad case of Tattle Tongue help him learn the difference between tattling and telling? This book provides a humorous, cleverly creative way to address the time-consuming tattling-related issues.

Don't Be Afraid to Drop
By Julia Cook
A book for anyone who is at a transitional point in their life by providing a positive perspective on change, taking risks, and giving back.

My Mom Thinks She's My Volleyball Coach...But She's Not!
By Julia Cook
This book, partnered by the USA Volleyball Association, informs parents how they can be supportive of their kids and their kids' teams without being pushy—and how to be their kid's biggest fans.

The Kid Trapper
By Julia Cook
In a non-offensive manner, *The Kid Trapper* takes the extremely sensitive issue of child-molestation and presents it in a way that gives the victim power and strength. It can be used to teach children and adults to recognize and prevent traps set by acquaintance molesters. This book can also be used as a diagnostic and therapy tool helping to relieve blame and guilt for both child and parent.

SCOOP
By Julia Cook
SCOOP is an acronym to help children remember five personal safety strategies to keep them safe. It helps equip children with safety skills to prevent child abduction, and is written in a non-threatening manner.